13HABITS.COM

The tale of
Tortoise Buffett and
Trader Hare

Available on
iTunes

The tale of Tortoise Buffett and Trader Hare
Shareholder Letters by Warren Buffett: www.berkshirehathaway.com/letters/letters.html
Story and Creative Direction by Lucas Remmerswaal: www.lucasremmerswaal.com
Original Art and illustrations by Annette Lodge: www.annettelodge.com
Concept development layout and design by Karl Fountaine: www.fountainedesign.co.nz

Title: The tale of Tortoise Buffett and Trader Hare
Author: Lucas Remmerswaal
Publisher: Lucas Remmerswaal
Address: 57 Crawford Cres, Kamo, Whangarei
ISBN-13: 978-1461015680
ISBN-10: 1461015685
LCCN: 2011904622

Noela
your love inspired me

The tale of Tortoise Buffett and Trader Hare

Introduction

During the financial crisis of 2008 Lucas Remmerswaal felt the pain!

He saw the hopelessness, regret, despair and tears in the eyes of retired people who had lost their life's savings. Being an idealist the question "What can I do about this tragedy?" haunted Remmerswaal for 2 years.

His answer – "I can share Warren Buffett's good habits with children." Inspired by Buffett's MBA speeches, example and wisdom – The tale of Tortoise Buffett and Trader Hare is a tribute to Warren Buffett on his 80th Birthday.

Good Habits are available for everyone to learn, adopt, and live by. Childhood is the place to start. Schools currently lack the resources to teach financial literacy. This series of entertaining and practical resources fill that gap. Parents and teachers will welcome these concise, witty and relevant books.

"The books are enchantingly clever, colorful and will draw any child's attention. They somehow bridge it between being too cutesy and being too hard to understand." Doris Buffett

"A child will want to pick this up. I don't care if they are 8 years old, 18 years old or 80 years old!" Beth Black (owner of The Book Worm, Omaha)

Once upon a time a
tortoise named Buffett,
who loved reading
and thinking things
through properly
before acting,

Tortoise Buffett→

and a hare
- let's call him Trader Hare -
who borrowed money to
invest short term, had an
argument about who could
make money grow fastest.

←Trader Hare

They decided to settle
the argument with a **race.**

"Well, heh heh, may the best man win..."

"I promise I won't beat you by too far, Tortoise Buffett!"

They agreed on a route
and started off the race.

Quicker than a flash, Trader Hare shot off
to borrow some money from the bank,
so he would have capital to invest.

Tortoise Buffett also wanted to invest.

But his investment capital came from the income he made by working hard. Really hard.

He sold coca-cola & chewing gum door to door, delivered newspapers, recycled golf balls, sold magazine subscriptions, and put pinball machines in barber shops.

He knew the way to win was having surplus income
to save to be able to invest...

Meanwhile, Trader Hare
had a great idea:
"Why not stop for lunch?"

He thought he was still
way ahead of the tortoise.

There was this wonderful
shady tree with soft green
grass underneath.
The whispering wind told
Trader Hare, "sleep, sleep!"

Tortoise Buffett, still working hard and investing with a purpose, passed the tree with the fluffy brown little bundle underneath and for a moment wished that he could join him.

However, he was a driven tortoise and knew
that this was his chance to win the race.
On his way he went, finished the race,
and emerged as the champ!

The Champ!
Slow and steady wins the
race every time.
↓

Trader Hare woke up with a shock
as he remembered he must repay the bank
before he could finish the race!

So he rushed to see his bank manager to pay back
the loan he had borrowed.
But in the meantime the stock market had crashed
and he was living beyond his means.
Trader Hare did not have enough money!

The bank made Trader Hare bankrupt just as he made a dash
for the finish line.....

...only to find the triumphant tortoise
waiting for him!

the beaten Trader Hare. →
Debt is a four letter word and
means a four word sentence -
Be Prepared for Trouble.

The moral of the story.

Slow and steady wins the race every time.
Tortoises read. Hares do not. Hares have no time to read!
Tortoises hate "debt" - hares love to scuttle to the bank
to "borrow" money! That is because they are
frantic by habit and are urged on by
this habit to rush, rush, and rush!

Tortoises always keep enough cash for six month's
living expenses in the bank. You must really want
to win with all of your heart!
Plan your race; do not ever
get side tracked.
Focus on your goal -
"the finishing line"!

And remember...

...good habits are the
basic tools that will determine
whether you are
a tortoise
or hare in life!

Warren Buffett, Billionaire businessman and <u>philanthropist</u>*
↓

"Warren Buffett is one of the best learning machines on this earth. The turtles which outrun the hares are learning machines.
If you stop learning in this world, the world rushes right by you."

Charlie Munger

*that means he gives away lots of his money to help others less fortunate!

Charlie Munger, Warren's right hand man.

"I insist on a lot of time being spent, almost every day, to just sit and think. That is very uncommon in American business. I read and think. So I do more reading and thinking, and make less impulse decisions than most people in business. I do it because I like this kind of life."

Warren Buffett

How Warren Buffett became a Billionaire

His father called him the "Fireball" — it must have been Warren's energy and enthusiasm! The first thing that Buffett's dad taught him was that the inner scorecard is much more important than the outer scorecard. His dad was a 100% inner scorecard guy. His father was a stockbroker. Buffett loved Saturday mornings when he was allowed to "mark the board" at his father's office. There was a shelf full of books. Buffett got into the habit of reading them, thinking and acting on the wisdom he discovered. Before starting out in business Buffett did his research collecting piles of soft drink bottle caps, which he sorted and counted before recording the numbers in a notebook. The numbers told him that Coca-Cola was the most popular soft drink. For his sixth birthday his dad gave him $20.00. That was just the beginning of his snowball. "My first business venture – was buying a six pack of Coke for 25 cents and selling each bottle for 5 cents." At Christmas he got a nickel-plated moneychanger from his aunt Alice. Buffett loved wearing it on his belt as it made him feel professional when he went around the neighborhood selling Coca-Cola and chewing gum. To make more money Buffett got up early each morning to deliver newspapers. He saved his money carefully.

By the age of nine he read and re-read "How to Win Friends and Influence People" by Dale Carnegie and he learned not to criticize condemn or complain. For his 10th Birthday, his dad took him on a trip to the east coast. Buffett was so excited! They went by train from Omaha, Nebraska, and he got to decide on the places to visit in New York City. When Buffett wanted to see the New York Stock Exchange he got to meet Sidney Weinberg. Buffett has never forgotten that first visit. It inspired him to get back to work with a passion. On his return to Omaha Buffett found a book in the Benson Library called "A Thousand Ways to Make a Thousand Dollars", in other words 'a million dollars'. As soon as he opened the book he was immediately hooked. Inside the front cover there was a tiny man with an enormous pile of coins and on the first page it said "Opportunity knocks". It had taken Buffett five years of work to save up $120.00. Buffett wanted to make even more money by investing his savings in the stock market so he could compound his money and make it grow!

At age 11, together with his older sister Doris his first partner, they bought three shares of Cities Service Preferred. That purchase cost them $114.75.

Buffett started out selling chewing gum and coca-cola door to door around the neighborhood, delivering newspapers, collecting waste paper and magazines for scrap, recycling used golf balls, working at a bakery, working as a clerk in his grandfather's grocery store, delivering groceries and shovelling snow. When Buffett was 12 his Dad was elected to congress, the family moved to Washington. There Buffett put ferocious energy into throwing three newspaper routes. All his effort was rewarded at the age of 13 when he got the opportunity to deliver The Washington Post, a morning paper, to a high class apartment complex, The Westchester — consisting of five buildings owned by Queen Wilhelmina of the Netherlands. Buffett started at 4.30am on a Sunday morning. The route included two other apartment buildings and a small route of single-family houses delivering hundreds of newspapers each day. Next he added a sideline business selling calendars and magazine subscriptions to his newspaper clients. After school he would deliver the Evening Star. By the age of 16 Buffett had accumulated more than $2,000 and he invested alongside his father in a hardware store, Builders Supply Co. Next Buffett bought himself a forty-acre farm that was worked by a tenant farmer in Thurston County, Nebraska. There was a business selling collectable stamps, a car-buffing enterprise and a pinball machine business. Buffett cleared old stocks of cornflakes, barbeques and dog biscuits. These were the first steps to becoming a Millionaire and later a Billionaire.

"I must have tried about 20 businesses by the time I graduated from high school. There's a study I've often quoted that shows that the best correlation with business success is the age at which you started your first business. The earlier, the better. I got half the investment capital I started with delivering newspapers."
Warren Buffett, Billionaire & Philanthropist.

Glossary

Borrow money You can borrow money from a Bank to buy an automobile, house or to buy or start a business. The borrower is really renting the bank's money for a fee called interest. This means that you pay back more money than you borrowed and this is how banks make their money.

Capital describes how much you are worth. When you add up the cash you have at home plus the money you have in the bank plus the valuable things you own the sum total of all these added together is your capital. Your capital is the money you have and the money you could raise by selling the things you own.

Businesses like Coca-Cola need capital to begin or expand production. The term capital describes the total sum that is needed to produce your favorite soft drinks.

Day Trader People that habitually buy and sell on the same day are called day traders. Some of the most commonly day-traded financial instruments are stocks, stock options and currencies.

Debt When you borrow money from a bank or a person it is called a debt. So a debt is simply when you owe money to someone else.

Family budget When your family decides to save money, the next step is to make a budget. A budget is a plan that estimates your income and expenses.

Your family should begin by estimating its total income per week or month then estimate its total expenses per week or month. To know how much you can save, take your income and minus your expenses, the amount left over is what your family will be able to save.

Home Loan Home buyers can rarely pay for the full cost of a house or home. Most must borrow a large part of the purchase price, pledging the house, lot and down payment as security to the bank. Pledging these things as security means if at some stage they are unable to pay back the loan, the bank can sell these things to get the money back.

Interest is a fee that is charged for borrowing money. It is usually a percentage of the amount you borrowed and is added to the total. So if you borrow $100 for 1 year and your interest is 10%, you will pay back $110.

Invest When you invest you are taking saving your money one step further. If you put your money into a business, this is called an investment. The money you have invested can help the business which can mean you make money or 'profit'. You invest with the hope of receiving a profit.

For short term investments you can invest your savings in the money market, corporate bonds and government notes.

For longer periods of time, say 5 to 10 years you can invest your savings in the share market. When you invest in stocks, they are businesses such as Coca-Cola that makes and sells your favorite drinks.

Loan When you want to buy or build a house and you do not have the large amount of money required to do so but you have saved enough money for the down payment, you may borrow the remainder of the money required to pay for the house from a bank.

Profit Profit is earned, when for example you buy a bottle of coke for $1 and sell it for $1.20 you have made a 20c profit.

Save One of the best things you can do with your money is save and invest it. When you save your money in a bank account the bank is then able to lend someone else money to buy a house or buy or start a business. This is how a bank makes money because the person who borrowed the money pays the bank back what they borrowed plus interest. If people don't save money, banks can't lend other people money and the economy wouldn't grow and flourish.

Billionaire
by Travie McCoy

I used to be a billionaire
called Bernie Mad
spending money that i never had
then i was on the cover of
New York magazine
Everyone I cheated hated me

Now every time I close my eyes
Leeroy winks and says "Goodnight"
And it would hit me every night
Oh I, I swear if I had just been fair
I'd still be a billionaire

Yeah, I was an investment broker
not actin like I's supposed ta
scheme idea from Ponzi
give Maddie your money
I'd probably still be runnin' my business
if it wasn't for the economy that
suddenly turned to sh*t

Give away a little dollar bait
people don't appreciate
money don't come easy but
you think so when you're greedy
It's been a couple of years since I've
been in prison
if I stopped I could learned
some useful lessons from Warren

Earn, invest then later you can spend it
the hare starts racing fast
but the tortoise will end it
Well make sure you don't forget about
me stupid
or history will repeat and we might as
well loop it

Now every time I close my eyes
Leeroy winks and says "Goodnight"
And it would hit me every night
Oh I, I swear if I had just been fair
I'd still be a billionaire

Oh, Oh......
Still be a billionaire
Oh, Oh....

Yeah I was just hiding all the evidence
Buying people presents
Some I gave to charity but
most was for my family
SEC took over 20 years to discover me
by then it looked like I had many times
just won the lootery

Yeah I was in a whole new tax bracket
But in recession it began to show the
cracks in it
If I took all the people lost and then
split it up
It would cost each one on earth around
10 bucks
Then with all of this money around me
They never thought I's lying
cause the sound of my jangling

I know we all have a similar dream
But to last as Billionaires takes more
than just some crazy scheme

I used to be a billionaire
called Bernie Mad
spending money that i never had
then i was on the cover of
New York magazine
Everyone I cheated hated me

Oh every time I close my eyes
Leeroy winks and says "Goodnight"
And it would hit me every night
Oh I, I swear if I had just been fair
I'd still be a billionaire

Oh, Oh....
Still be a billionaire
Oh, Oh....

I used to be a billionaire called Bernie
Mad

http://www.youtube.com/watch?v=sd1ml1jn-po

Thank You

To Warren Buffett for making his Shareholders letters freely available. To the students and teachers at Hurupaki Primary and Kamo Intermediate School in Whangarei who generously gave their time to support this project, to them I am truly grateful.

I am especially thankful to my wife Noela, my children, my father, my family, Annette Lodge, Prof. John Hattie, Karl Fountaine and the team at Amazon.com.

8749046R0

Made in the USA
Charleston, SC
10 July 2011